A Note to Parents and Caregivers:

Read-it! Readers are for children who are just starting on the amazing road to reading. These beautiful books support both the acquisition of reading skills and the love of books.

 The PURPLE LEVEL presents basic topics and objects using high frequency words and simple language patterns.

 The RED LEVEL presents familiar topics using common words and repeating sentence patterns.

 The BLUE LEVEL presents new ideas using a larger vocabulary and varied sentence structure.

 The YELLOW LEVEL presents more challenging ideas, a broad vocabulary, and wide variety in sentence structure.

 The GREEN LEVEL presents more complex ideas, an extended vocabulary range, and expanded language structures.

 The ORANGE LEVEL presents a wide range of ideas and concepts using challenging vocabulary and complex language structures.

When sharing a book with your child, read in short stretches, pausing often to talk about the pictures. Have your child turn the pages and point to the pictures and familiar words. And be sure to reread favorite stories or parts of stories.

There is no right or wrong way to share books with children. Find time to read with your child, and pass on the legacy of literacy.

Adria F. Klein, Ph.D.
Professor Emeritus
California State University
San Bernardino, California

First American edition published in 2005 by
Picture Window Books
5115 Excelsior Boulevard
Suite 232
Minneapolis, MN 55416
877-845-8392
www.picturewindowbooks.com

First published in Canada in 1999 by
Les éditions Héritage inc.
300 Arran Street, Saint Lambert
Quebec, Canada J4R 1K5

Printed in the United States of America.

Library of Congress Cataloging-in-Publication Data
Hébert, Marie-Francine.
John's day / author, Marie-Francine Hébert ; illustrator, Caroline Hamel.
p. cm. — (Read-it! readers)
Summary: After John is scolded for running like a horse, wiggling like a monkey, and
singing like a bird, he puts all the animals away in his mind and they must come out to
play in his dreams.
ISBN 1-4048-1071-4 (hardcover)
[1. Behavior—Fiction. 2. Day—Fiction. 3. Animal behavior—Fiction. 4. Dreams—
Fiction.] I. Hamel, Caroline, ill. II. Title. III. Series.

PZ7.H3527Jo 2004
[E]—dc22
                                                                    2004025110

John's Day

By Marie-Francine Hébert
Illustrated by Caroline Hamel

Special thanks to our advisers for their expertise:

Adria F. Klein, Ph.D.
Professor Emeritus, California State University
San Bernardino, California

Susan Kesselring, M.A.
Literacy Educator
Rosemount - Apple Valley - Eagan (Minnesota) School District

PICTURE WINDOW BOOKS
Minneapolis, Minnesota

4

John does not understand why, every time he runs through the house, Daddy uses his grumpy bear voice.
"Enough horsing around! You're not on a racetrack!" Daddy yells.

John imagines grabbing a horse by its mane and bringing it back in the stable.

John does not understand why, every time he sings in the house, Mommy rushes in like a lioness and says,

"You cannot sing at the top of your lungs, my little bird. You will disturb the whole neighborhood."

John imagines shutting the bird's beak and putting it in a cage.

7

John does not understand why his sister changes moods like a chameleon changes color. As soon as one of her friends shows up, she gets crabby and says, "Quit following me like a puppy dog!"

John imagines putting a dog on a leash and laying him down in a doghouse.

John pays a visit to Grandma. He doesn't run, shout, or follow her like a puppy dog. He is as quiet as a little cat.

John does not understand why Grandma howls like a scared wolf and says, "Do you want to kill me? Get down from that tree right away, my kitty."

John imagines putting the cat in a basket.

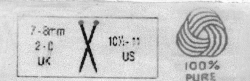

Yippee! John found the answer to the question before everyone else. He doesn't understand why the teacher tells him, "Stop wiggling like a monkey! You're disturbing the whole class."

John imagines rolling up the monkey in its long tail and sending it for a timeout.

13

How quiet John is! "He's as quiet as a picture!" says Daddy, Mommy, big sister, Grandma, and the teacher.

The truth is, John is daydreaming.

His body is awake, but in his head everything is asleep: the horse, the bird, the dog, the cat, the monkey, and everything else.

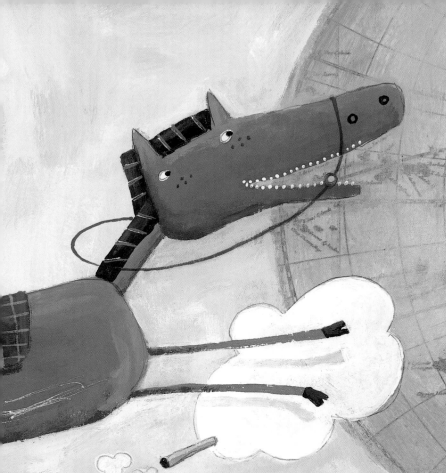

When night comes, John goes to bed. As soon as John's body falls asleep, the animals in his head wake up.

The horse escapes from its stable. It gallops into the country, jumps over a ditch, and goes through a river. Uh, oh! The sea! The horse jumps so high it lands on a cloud. There it stays for a trip around the world.

17

18

The bird flies away from its cage, chirping. "Cock-a-doodle-doo!" answers the neighbor's rooster.

Just then, the hens begin to dance, and the chicks hatch from their eggshells, keeping the beat. There is a party in the henhouse.

The dog runs out of his doghouse, barking.
"Hurry, a little girl just fell in the river!"
Like a good dog, it jumps in the water and
brings the child to the shore just in time.
The dog is a hero now.

4310

22

The cat leaves its basket, looking for Grandma to bring her ball of yarn back. It walks around the house, climbs onto the window frame, and then onto the roof.

Finally, it sees Grandma. But where could the yarn be? It's wrapped around the house!

"What a wonderful idea! Now winter can come," says Grandma.

The monkey steps out of the corner. Under the circus tent, it moves forward to do its trick. "Attention, everyone!" the monkey yells.

24

He throws himself up in the air and catches himself with his tail. All the members of the audience clap, even the teacher.

Uh, oh! The sun is up. John will wake up soon. All the animals go back to their homes. The horse goes in its stable, the bird in its cage, the dog in its doghouse, the cat in its basket, and the monkey in its corner.

1.

3.

4.

5.

1-2.a-3.b-4.e-5.d 27

What does John see through the window?
Daddy is coming back as a bear. Mommy, the
lioness, is sneaking back from behind the far
away bush. His sister, the chameleon, is
making her way through the garden hidden
by the fog.

Who's walking around like a wolf watching over her cubs? Grandma! But who's jumping and splashing in the pond?

The teacher is late this morning. Oh! Here she comes with a bit of dream in her eyes and a lily pad in her hair, still wet. Everyone laughs—even the teacher. John understands.

Anything is possible in dreams.

More *Read-it!* Readers

Bright pictures and fun stories help you practice your reading skills. Look for more books at your level.

A Clown in Love by Mireille Villeneuve
Alex and the Game of the Century by Gilles Tibo
Alex and Toolie by Gilles Tibo
Daddy's an Alien by Bruno St-Aubin
Emily Lee Carole Temblay
Forrest and Freddy by Gilles Tibo
Gabby's School by the Sea by Marie-Danielle Croteau
Grampy's Bad Day by Dominique Demers
John's Day by Marie-Francine Hébert
Peppy, Patch, and the Postman by Marisol Sarrazin
Peppy, Patch, and the Socks by Marisol Sarrazin
The Princess and the Frog by Margaret Nash
Rachel's Adventure Ring by Sylvia Roberge Blanchet
Run! by Sue Ferraby
Sausages! by Anne Adeney
Stickers, Shells, and Snow Globes by Dana Meachen Rau
Theodore the Millipede by Carole Tremblay
The Truth About Hansel and Gretel by Karina Law
When Nobody's Looking... by Louise Tondreau-Levert

Looking for a specific title or level? A complete list of *Read-it!* Readers is available on our Web site: *www.picturewindowbooks.com*